I0818645

# *Traders Risk*

# *Traders Risk*

Roger Dee

ÆGYPAN PRESS

From *Galaxy Science Fiction,* February, 1958.

Special thanks to Greg Weeks, Stephen Blundell, and the Online Distributed Proofreading Team (which can be found at http://www.pgdp.net).

*Traders Risk*
A publication of
ÆGYPAN PRESS

www.aegypan.com

*Keeping this cargo meant death — to jettison it meant to make flotsam and jetsam of a world!*

The Ciriimian ship was passing in hyperdrive through a classic three-body system, comprising in this case a fiercely white sun circled by a fainter companion and a single planet that swung in precise balance, when the Canthorian Zid broke out of its cage in the specimen hold.

Of the ship's social quartet, Chafis One and Two were asleep at the moment, dreaming wistful dreams of conical Ciriimian cities spearing up to a soft and plum-colored sky. The Zid raged into their communal rest cell, smashed them down from their gimbaled sleeping perches and, with the ravening blood-hunger of its kind, devoured them before they could wake enough to teleport to safety.

Chafis Three and Four, on psi shift in the forward control cubicle, might have fallen as easily if the mental screamings of their fellows had not warned them in time. As it was, they had barely time to teleport themselves to the after hold, as far as possible from immediate danger, and to consider the issue while the Zid lunged about the ship in search of them with malignant cries and a great shrieking of claws on metal.

Their case was the more desperate because the Chafis were professional freighters with little experience of emergency. Hauling a Zid from Canthorian jungles to a Ciriimian zoo was a prosaic enough assignment so long as the cage held, but with the raging brute swiftly smelling them out, they were helpless to catch and restrain it.

When the Zid found them, they had no other course but to teleport back to the control cubicle and wait until the beast should snuff them down again. The Zid learned quickly, so quickly that it was soon clear that its physical strength would far outlast their considerable but limited telekinetic ability.

Still they possessed their share of owlish Ciriimian logic and hit soon enough upon the one practical course – to jettison the Zid on the nearest world demonstrably free of intelligent life.

They worked hurriedly, between jumps fore and aft. Chafi Three, while they were still in the control cubicle, threw the ship out of hyperdrive within scant miles of the neighboring sun's single planet. Chafi Four, on the next jump, scanned the ship's charts and identified the system through which they traveled.

Luck was with them. The system had been catalogued some four Ciriimian generations before and tagged: *Planet undeveloped. Tranquil marine intelligences only.*

The discovery relieved them greatly for the reason that no Ciriimian, even to save his own feathered skin, would have set down such a monster as the Zid among rational but vulnerable entities.

The planet was a water world, bare of continents and only sparsely sprinkled with minor archipelagoes. The islands suited the Chafis' purpose admirably.

"The Zid does not swim," Chafi Four radiated. "Marooned, it can do no harm to marine intelligences."

"Also," Chafi Three pointed out as they dodged to the control cubicle again just ahead of the slavering Zid, "we may return later with a Canthorian hunting party and recover our investment."

Closing their perception against the Zid's distracting ragings, they set to work with perfect coordination.

Chafi Three set down the ship on an island that was only one of a freckling chain of similar islands. Chafi Four projected himself first to the opened port; then, when the Zid charged after him, to the herbivore-cropped sward of tropical setting outside.

The Zid lunged out. Chafi Four teleported inside again. Chafi Three closed the port. Together they relaxed their perception shields in relief –

Unaware in their consternation that they committed the barbarous lapse of vocalizing, they twittered aloud when they realized the extent of their error.

Above the far, murmurous whisper of expected marine cerebration there rose an uncoordinated mishmash of thought from at least two strong and relatively complex intelligences.

"Gas-breathing!" Chafi Four said unbelievingly. "Warm-blooded, land-dwelling, mammalian!"

"A Class Five culture," Chafi agreed shakenly. His aura quivered with the shock of betrayal. "The catalogue was *wrong.*"

Ironically, their problem was more pressing now than before. Unless checked, the Zid would rapidly depopulate the island – and, to check it, they must break a prime rule of Galactic protocol in asking the help of a new and untested species.

But they had no choice. They teleported at once into the presence of the two nearby natives – and met with frustration beyond Ciriimian experience.

Jeff Aubray glimpsed the Ciriimian ship's landing because the morning was a Oneday, and on Onedays his mission to the island demanded that he be up and about at sunrise.

For two reasons: On Onedays, through some unfailing miracle of Calaxian seamanship, old Charlie Mack sailed down in his ancient *Island Queen* from the township that represented colonial Terran civilization in Procynian Archipelago 147, bringing supplies and gossip to last Jeff through the following Tenday. The *Queen* would dock at Jeff's little pier at dawn; she was never late.

Also on Onedays, necessarily before Charlie Mack's visit, Jeff must assemble his smuggled communicator – kept dismantled and hidden from suspicious local eyes – and report to Earth Interests Consulate his progress during the cycle just ended. The ungodly hour of transmission, naturally, was set to coincide with the closing of the Consul's field office halfway around the planet.

So the nacreous glory of Procyon's rising was just tinting the windows of Jeff's cottage when he aligned and activated his little communicator on his breakfast table. Its three-inch screen lighted to signal and a dour and disappointed Consul Satterfield looked at him. Behind Satterfield, foreshortened to gnomishness by the pickup, lurked Dr. Hermann, Earth Interests' resident zoologist.

"No progress," Jeff reported, "except that the few islanders I've met seem to be accepting me at last. A little more time and they might let me into the Township, where I can learn something. If Homeside – "

"You've had seven Tendays," Satterfield said. "Homeside won't wait longer, Aubray. They need those calm-crystals too badly."

"They'll use force?" Jeff had considered the possibility, but its immediacy appalled him. "Sir, these colonists had been autonomous for over two hundred years, ever since the Fourth War cut them off from us. Will Homeside deny their independence?"

His sense of loss at Satterfield's grim nod stemmed from something deeper than sympathy for the islanders. It found roots in his daily rambles over the little island granted him by the Township for the painting he had begun as a blind to his assignment, and in the gossip of old Charlie Mack and the few others he had met. He had learned to appreciate the easy life of the islands well enough to be dismayed now by what must happen under EI pressure to old Charlie and his handful of sun-browned fisherfolk.

Unexpectedly, because Jeff had not considered that it might matter, he was disturbed by the realization that he wouldn't be seeing Jennifer, old Charlie Mack's red-haired niece, once occupation began. Jennifer, who sailed with her uncle and did a crewman's work as a matter of course, would despise the sight of him.

The Consul's pessimism jolted Jeff back to the moment at hand.

"Homeside will deny their autonomy, Aubray. I've had a warp-beam message today ordering me to move in."

The situation was desperate enough at home, Jeff had to admit. Calaxian calm-crystals did what no refinement of Terran therapeutics had been able to manage. They erased the fears of the neurotic and calmed the quiverings of the hypertensive – both in alarming majority in the shattering aftermath of the Fourth War – with no adverse effects at all. Permanent benefit was slow but cumulative, offering for the first time a real step toward ultimate stability. The medical, psychiatric and political fields cried out for crystals and more crystals.

"If the islanders would tell us their source and let us help develop it," Satterfield said peevishly, "instead of doling out a handful of crystals every Tenday, there wouldn't be any need of action. Homeside feels they're just letting us have some of the surplus."

"Not likely," Jeff said. "They don't use the crystals themselves."

Old Dr. Hermann put his chin almost on the Consul's shoulder to present his wizened face to the scanner.

"Of course they don't," he said. "On an uncomplicated, even simple-minded world like this, who would need crystals? But maybe they fear glutting the market or the domination of outside capital coming in to develop the source. When people backslide, there's no telling what's on their minds and we have no time to waste negotiating or convincing them. In any case, how could they stop us from moving in?" Abruptly he switched to his own interest. "Aubray, have you learned anything new about the Scoops?"

"Nothing beyond the fact that the islanders don't talk about them," Jeff said. "I've seen perhaps a dozen offshore during the seven cycles I've been here. One usually surfaces outside my harbor at about the time old Charlie Mack's supply boat comes in."

Thinking of Charlie Mack brought a forced end to his report. "Charlie's due now. I'll call back later."

He cut the circuit, hurrying to have his communicator stowed away before old Charlie's arrival – not, he thought bitterly, that being found out now would make any great difference.

Stepping out into the brief Calaxian dawn, he caught his glimpse of the Ciriimian ship's landing before the island forest of palm-ferns cut it off from sight. Homeside hadn't been bluffing, he thought, assuming as a matter of course that this was the task force Satterfield had been ordered to send.

"They didn't waste any time," Jeff growled. "Damn them."

He ignored the inevitable glory of morning rainbow that just preceded Procyon's rising and strode irritably down to his miniature dock. He was still scowling over what he should tell Charlie Mack when the *Island Queen* hove into view.

She was a pretty sight. There was an artist's perception in Jeff in spite of his drab years of EI patrol duty; the white puff of sail on dark-green sea, gliding across calm water banded with lighter and darker striae where submerged shoals lay, struck something responsive in him. The comparison it forced between Calaxia and Earth, whose yawning Fourth War scars and heritage of anxieties made calm-crystals so desperately necessary, oppressed him. Calaxia was wholly unscarred, her people without need of the calm-crystals they traded.

Something odd in the set of the *Queen's* sails puzzled him until he identified the abnormality. In spite of distance and the swift approach of the old fishing boat, he could have sworn that her sails bellied not with the wind, but against.

They fell slack, however, when the *Queen* reached his channel and flapped lazily, reversing to catch the wind and nose her cautiously into the shallows. Jeff dismissed it impatiently—a change of wind or some crafty maneuver of old Charlie Mack's to take advantage of the current.

Jeff had just set foot on his dock when it happened. Solid as the planking itself, and all but blocking off his view of the nearing *Island Queen,* stood a six-foot owl.

It was wingless and covered smoothly with pastel-blue feathers. It stood solidly on carefully manicured yellow feet and stared at him out of square violet eyes.

Involuntarily he took a backward step, caught his heel on a sun-warped board and sat down heavily.

"Well, what the devil!" he said inanely.

The owl winced and disappeared without a sound.

Jeff got up shakily and stumbled to the dock's edge. A chill conviction of insanity gripped him when he looked down on water lapping smooth and undisturbed below.

"I've gone mad," he said aloud.

Out on the bay, another catastrophe just as improbable was in progress.

Old Charlie Mack's *Island Queen* had veered sharply off course, left the darker-green stripe of safe channel and plunged into water too shallow for her draft. The boat heeled on shoal sand, listed and hung aground with wind-filled sails holding her fast.

The Scoop that had surfaced just behind her was so close that Jeff wondered if its species' legendary good nature had been misrepresented. It floated like a glistening plum-colored island, flat dorsal flippers undulating gently on the water and its great filmy eyes all but closed against the slanting glare of morning sun.

It was more than vast. The thing must weigh, Jeff thought dizzily, thousands or maybe millions of tons.

He thought he understood the *Queen's* grounding when he saw the swimmer stroking urgently toward his dock. Old Charlie had abandoned his boat and was swimming in to escape the Scoop.

But it wasn't Charlie. It was Jennifer, Charlie's niece.

Jeff took the brown hand she put up and drew her to the dock beside her, steadying her while she shook out her dripping red hair and regained her breath. Seawater had plastered Jennifer's white blouse and knee-length dungarees to her body like a second skin, and the effect bordered on the spectacular.

"Did you see it?" she demanded.

Jeff wrestled his eyes away to the Scoop that floated like a purple island in the bay.

"A proper monster," he said. "You got out just in time."

She looked at once startled and impatient. "Not the Scoop, you idiot. The owl."

It was Jeff's turn to stare. "Owl? There was one on the dock, but I thought – "

"So did I." She sounded relieved. "But if you saw one, too. . . . All of a sudden, it was standing there on deck beside me, right out of nowhere. I lost my head and grounded the *Queen,* and it vanished. The owl, I mean."

"So did mine," Jeff said.

While they stood marveling, the owls came back.

Chafis Three and Four were horribly shaken by the initial attempt at communication with the natives. Nothing in Ciriimian experience had prepared them for creatures intelligent but illogical, individually perceptive yet isolated from each other.

"Communication by audible symbol," Chafi Three said. He ruffled his feathers in a shudder. "Barbarous!"

"Atavistic," agreed Chafi Four. "They could even *lie* to each other."

But their dilemma remained. They must warn the natives before the prowling Zid found them, else there would be no natives.

"We must try again," Three concluded, "searching out and using the proper symbols for explanation."

"Vocally," said Chafi Four.

They shuddered and teleported.

The sudden reappearance of his hallucination – doubled – startled Jeff no more than the fact that he seemed to be holding Jennifer Mack tightly. Amazingly, his immediate problem was not the possibility of harm from the owls, but whether he should reassure Jennifer before or after releasing her.

He compromised by leaving the choice to her. "They can't be dangerous," he said. "There are no land-dwelling predators on Calaxia. I read that in – "

"Nothing like *that* ever hatched out on Calaxia," said Jennifer. She pulled free of him. "If they're real, they came from somewhere else."

The implication drew a cold finger down Jeff's spine. "That would mean other cultures out here. And in all our years of planet-hunting, we haven't found one."

Memory chilled him further.

"A ship landed inland a few minutes ago," he said. "I took it for an EI consulate craft, but it could have been – "

The Ciriimians caught his mental image of the landing and intervened while common ground offered.

"The ship was ours," said Chafi Three. He had not vocalized since fledgling days and his voice had a jarring croak of disuse. "Our Zid escaped its cage and destroyed two of us, forcing us to maroon it here for our own safety. Unfortunately, we trusted our star manual's statement that the planet is unpopulated."

The Terrans drew together again.

"Zid?" Jeff echoed.

Chafi Four relieved his fellow of the strain by trying his own rusty croak. "A vicious Canthorian predator, combing the island at this moment for prey. You must help us to recapture it."

"So that you may identify it," Chafi Three finished helpfully, "the Zid has this appearance."

His psi projection of the Zid appeared on the dock before them with demoniac abruptness – crouched to leap, twin tails lashing and its ten-foot length bristling with glassy magenta bristles. It had a lethal pair of extra limbs that sprang from the shoulders to end in taloned seizing-hands, and its slanted red eyes burned malevolently from a snouted, razor-fanged face.

It was too real to bear. Jeff stepped back on suddenly unreliable legs. Jennifer fainted against him and the unexpected weight of her sent them both sprawling to the dock.

"We lean on weak reeds," Chafi Three said. "Creatures who collapse with terror at the mere projection of a Zid can be of little assistance in recapturing one."

Chafi Four agreed reluctantly. "Then we must seek aid elsewhere."

When Jeff Aubray pulled himself up from the planking, the apparitions were gone. His knees shook and perspiration crawled cold on his face, but he managed to haul Jennifer up with him.

"Come out of it, will you?" he yelled ungallantly in her ear. "If a thing like that is loose on the island, we've got to get help!"

Jennifer did not respond and he slapped her, until her eyes fluttered angrily.

"There's an EI communicator in my cabin," Jeff said. "Let's go."

Memory lent Jennifer a sudden vitality that nearly left Jeff behind in their dash for the cottage up the beach.

"The door," Jeff panted, inside. "Fasten the hurricane bolt. Hurry."

While she secured the flimsy door, he ripped through his belongings, aligning his EI communicator again on his breakfast table. Finding out where the islanders got their calm-crystals had become suddenly unimportant; just then, he wanted nothing so much as to see a well-armed patrol ship nosing down out of the Calaxian sunrise.

He was activating the screen when Jennifer, in a magnificent rage in spite of soaked blouse and dungarees, advanced on him.

"You're an Earth Interests spy after all," she accused. "They said in the Township you are no artist, but Uncle Charlie and I – "

Jeff made a pushing motion. "Keep away from me. Do you want that devil tearing the cabin down around us?"

She fell quiet, remembering the Zid, and he made his call. "Aubray, Chain 147. Come in, Consulate!"

There was a sound of stealthy movement outside the cabin and he flicked sweat out of his eyes with a hand that shook.

"EI, for God's sake, come in! I'm in trouble here!"

The image on his three-inch screen was not Consul Satterfield's but the startled consulate operator's. "Trouble?"

Jeff forced stumbling words into line. The EI operator shook his head doubtfully.

"Consul's gone for the day, Aubray. I'll see if I can reach him."

"He was about to send out an EI patrol ship to take over here in the islands," Jeff said. "Tell him to hurry it!"

He knew when he put down the microphone that the ship would be too late. EI might still drag the secret of the calm-crystal source out of the islanders, but Jeff Aubray and Jennifer Mack wouldn't be on hand to witness their sorry triumph. The flimsy cabin could not stand for long against the sort of brute the owls had shown him, and there was no sort of weapon at hand. They couldn't even run.

"There's something outside," Jennifer said in a small voice.

Her voice seemed to trigger the attack.

The Zid lunged against the door with a force that cracked the wooden hurricane bolt across and opened a three-inch slit between leading edge and lintel. Jeff had a glimpse of slanted red eyes and white-fanged snout before reflex sent him headlong to shoulder the door shut again.

"The bunk," he panted at Jennifer. "Shove it over."

Between them, they wedged the bunk against the door and held it in place. Then they stood looking palely at each other and waiting for the next attack.

It came from a different quarter – the wide double windows that overlooked the bay. The Zid, rearing upright, smashed away the flimsy rattan blinds with a taloned seizing-hand and looked redly in at them.

Like a man in a dream, Jeff caught up his communicator from the table and hurled it. The Zid caught it deftly, sank glistening teeth into the unit and demolished it with a single snap.

Crushed, the rig's powerful little battery discharged with a muffled sputtering and flashing of sparks. The Zid howled piercingly and dropped away from the window.

That gave Jeff time enough to reach the storm shutters and secure them – only to rush again with Jennifer to their bunk barricade as the Zid promptly renewed its ferocious attack on the door.

He flinched when Jennifer, to be heard above the Zid's ragings, shouted in his ear: "My Scoop should have the *Queen* afloat by now. Can we reach her?"

"Scoop?" The Zid's avid cries discouraged curiosity before it was well born. "We'd never make it. We couldn't possibly outrun that beast."

The Zid crashed against the door and drove it inches ajar, driving back their barricade. One taloned paw slid in and slashed viciously at random. Jeff ducked and strained his weight against the bunk, momentarily pinning the Zid's threshing forelimb.

Chafi Three chose that moment to reappear, nearly causing Jeff to let go the bunk and admit the Zid.

"Your female's suggestion is right," the Ciriimian croaked. "The Zid does not swim. Four and I are arranging escape on that premise."

The Zid's talons ripped through the door, leaving parallel rows of splintered breaks. Both slanted red eyes glared in briefly.

"Then you'd damn well better hurry," Jeff panted. The door, he estimated, might – or might not – hold for two minutes more.

The Ciriimian vanished. There was a slithering sound in the distance that sounded like a mountain in motion, and with it a stertorous grunting that all but drowned out the Zid's cries. Something nudged the cottage with a force that all but knocked it flat.

"*My Scoop!*" Jennifer exclaimed. She let go the barricade and ran to the window to throw open the storm shutters. "Never mind the door. This way, quick!"

She scrambled to the windowsill and jumped. Numbly, Jeff saw her suspended there, feet only inches below the sill, apparently on empty air. Then the door sagged again under the Zid's lungings and he left the bunk to follow Jennifer.

He landed on something tough and warm and slippery, a monstrous tail fluke that stretched down the beach to merge into a flat purplish acreage of back, forested with endless rows of fins and spines and enigmatic tendrils. The Scoop, he saw, and only half believed it, had wallowed into the shallows alongside his dock. It had reversed its unbelievable length to keep the head submerged, and at the same time had backed out of the water until its leviathan tail spanned the hundred-odd yards of sloping beach from surf to cabin.

Just ahead of him, Jennifer caught an erect fin-spine and clung with both arms. "Hang on! We're going – "

The Scoop contracted itself with a suddenness that yanked them yards from the cottage and all but dislodged Jeff. Beyond the surf, the shallows boiled whitely where the Scoop fought for traction to draw its grounded bulk into the water.

Jeff looked back once to see the Zid close the distance between and spring upward to the tail fluke behind him. He had an instant conviction that the brute's second spring would see him torn to bits, but the Scoop at the moment found water deep enough to move in earnest. The Zid could only sink in all six taloned limbs and hold fast.

The hundred-odd yards from cabin to beach passed in a blur of speed. The Scoop reached deeper water and submerged, throwing a mountainous billow that sent the *Island Queen* reeling and all but foundered her.

Jeff was dislodged instantly and sank like a stone.

He came up, spouting water and fighting for breath, to find himself a perilous twenty feet from the Zid. The Zid, utterly out of its element, screamed hideously and threshed water to froth, all its earlier ferocity vanished under the imminent and unfamiliar threat of drowning. Jeff sank again and churned desperately to put distance between them.

He came up again, nearly strangled, to find that either he or the Zid had halved the distance between them. They were all but eye to eye when Jennifer caught him and towed him away toward the doubtful safety of the *Island Queen.*

Chafis Three and Four appeared from nowhere and stood solemnly by while the Zid weakened and sank with a final gout of bubbles.

"We must have your friend's help," Chafi Three said to Jennifer then, "to recover our investment."

Jeff wheeled on him incredulously. "*Me* go down there after that monster? Not on your – "

"He means the Scoop," Jennifer said. "They brought it ashore to help us out of the cabin. Why shouldn't it help them now?"

The Scoop came up out of the water so smoothly that the *Island Queen* hardly rocked, dangling the limp form of the Zid from its great rubbery lips like a drowned kitten.

"Here," Jennifer said.

The Scoop touched its vast face to the *Queen's* rail and dropped the unconscious body to the deck. The Zid twitched weakly and coughed up froth and water.

Jeff backed away warily. "Damn it, are we going through all that again? Once it gets its wind back – "

Chafi Three interrupted him this time. "The crystal now. We must have it to quiet the Zid until it is safely caged again."

Jennifer turned suddenly firm. "No. I won't let this EI informer know about that."

The Ciriimians were firmer.

"It will not matter now. Galactic Adjustment will extend aid to both Calaxia and Terra, furnishing substitutes for the crystals you deal in. There will be no loss to either faction."

"No loss?" Jennifer repeated indignantly. "But then there won't be any demand for our crystals! We'll lose everything we've gained."

"Not so," Chafi Three assured her. "Galactic will offer satisfactory items in exchange, as well as a solution to Terra's problems."

The Scoop, sensing Jennifer's surrender, slid its ponderous bulk nearer and opened its mouth, leaving half an acre of lower jaw resting flush with the *Island Queen's* deck. Without hesitation, Jennifer stepped over the rail and vanished into the yawning pinkish cavern beyond.

Appalled, Jeff rushed after her. "Jennifer! Have you lost your mind?"

"There is no danger," Chafi Three assured him. "Scoops are benevolent as well as intelligent, and arrived long ago at a working agreement with the islanders. This one has produced a crystal and is ready to be relieved of it, else it would not have attached itself to a convenient human."

Jeff said dizzily, "The Scoops make the crystals?"

"There is a nidus just back of a fleshy process in its throat, corresponding to your own tonsils, which produces a crystal much as your Terran oyster secretes a pearl. The irritation distracts the Scoops from their meditations – they are a philosophical species, though not mechanically progressive – and prompts them to barter their strength for a time to be rid of it."

Jennifer reappeared with a walnut-sized crystal in her hand and vaulted across the rail.

"There goes another Scoop," she said resignedly. "The *Queen* will have to tack with the wind for a while until another one shows up."

"So that's why your sails bellied backward when you came in to harbor," said Jeff. "The thing was *towing* you."

A thin, high streak of vapor-trail needling down toward them from the sunrise rainbow turned the channel of his thought.

"That will be Satterfield and his task force," Jeff told the Chafis. "I think you're going to find yourselves in an argument over that matter of squeezing Terra out of the crystal trade."

They reassured him solemnly.

"Terra has no real need of the crystals. We can offer a tested genetics program that will eliminate racial anxiety within a few generations, and supply neural therapy equipment – on a trade basis, of course – that will serve the crystals' purpose during the interim."

There should be a flaw somewhere, Jeff felt, but he failed to see one. He gave up trying when he found Jennifer eying him with uncharacteristic uncertainty.

"You'll be glad to get back to your patrol work," she said. It had an oddly tentative sound.

Somehow the predictable monotony of consulate work had never seemed less inviting. The prospect of ending his Calaxian tour and going back to a half-barren and jittery Earth appealed to Jeff even less.

"No," he said. "I'd like to stay."

"There's nothing to do but fish and sail around looking for Scoops ready to shed their crystals," Jennifer reminded him. "Still, Uncle Charlie has talked about settling in the Township and standing for Council election. Can you fish and sail, Jeff Aubray?"

The consulate rocket landed ashore, but Jeff ignored it.

"I can learn," he said.

– ROGER DEE

www.ingramcontent.com/pod-product-compliance
Lightning Source LLC
Chambersburg PA
CBHW030416310726
48979CB00002B/438

* 9 7 8 1 4 6 3 8 9 5 0 6 8 *